dick bruna

miffy goes to stay

SIMON AND SCHUSTER
London   New York   Sydney   Toronto   New Delhi

A letter came for Miffy

asking her to stay.

Her friend was hoping that she'd come

to visit her and play.

This was new to Miffy –

travelling on her own.

Mother took her to the bus

but Miff got on alone.

The bus set off along the road

then at her journey's end

Miff looked out the window

to see her waiting friend.

Hi there, Miffy, called her friend,

I'm so glad that you're here.

Her mother smiled at Miffy.

How nice to see you, dear.

At first the only thing they did

was sit and chat and smile,

as Miffy hadn't seen her friend

for really quite a while.

But then they played at hide-and-seek

and that went really well.

With lots of trees to hide behind,

where's Miffy? Can you tell?

Next they ran across the grass

playing 'can't catch me'.

Which of them is chasing here?

See if you can see.

Then they got the roller skates.

For Miffy this was new.

You go first, said Miffy

and show me what to do.

When Miffy tried she found

it wasn't easy, not at all.

But though it was so tricky

she managed not to fall.

That afternoon they played indoors

at scissor-cutting crafts.

Miffy's nearly finished hers –

they're making paper masks.

At night they had their bath together.

That was really fun.

The two of them were soaking wet

before their bath was done.

And then at last they went to bed

and soon were sleeping too,

for there had been so many things

to play at, say and do.

Original title: nijntje gaat logeren
Original text Dick Bruna © copyright Mercis Publishing bv, 1988
Illustrations Dick Bruna © copyright Mercis bv, 1988
This edition published in Great Britain in 2017 by Simon and Schuster UK Limited
Publication licensed by Mercis Publishing bv, Amsterdam
English translation by Tony Mitton, 2017
ISBN 978 1 4711 2337 5
Printed and bound by SDP SachsenDruck GmbH, Germany

www.simonandschuster.co.uk

MIX

From responsible
sources

FSC® C021195